Pretzel and the Puppies

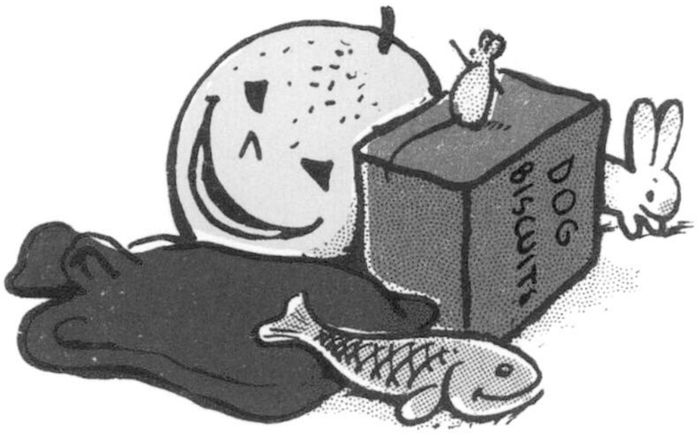
DOG BISCUITS

by

Margret & H. A. Rey

Houghton Mifflin Harcourt
Boston New York

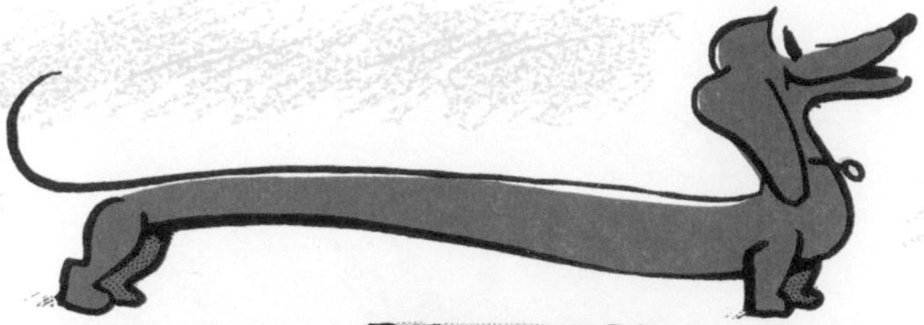

This is **PRETZEL**,
the longest dachshund in the world.
He can do many things because he is so long,
but it does not always turn out well...

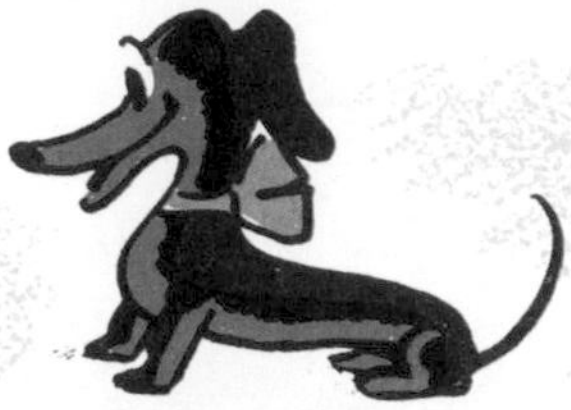

This is **GRETA**, Pretzel's wife.
She sometimes has to straighten things out
when Pretzel gets into trouble.

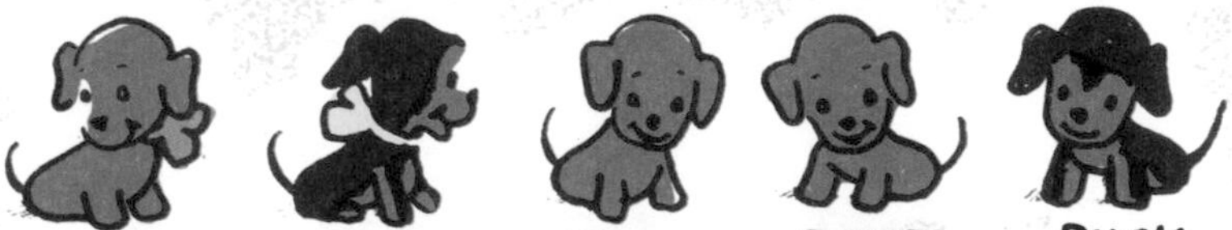

POLLY PENNY PAT PETE PUCK

These are the **PUPPIES**
(two girls and three boys), who love to
play with their Daddy.

And if you want to know more about Pretzel –

– just turn the page!

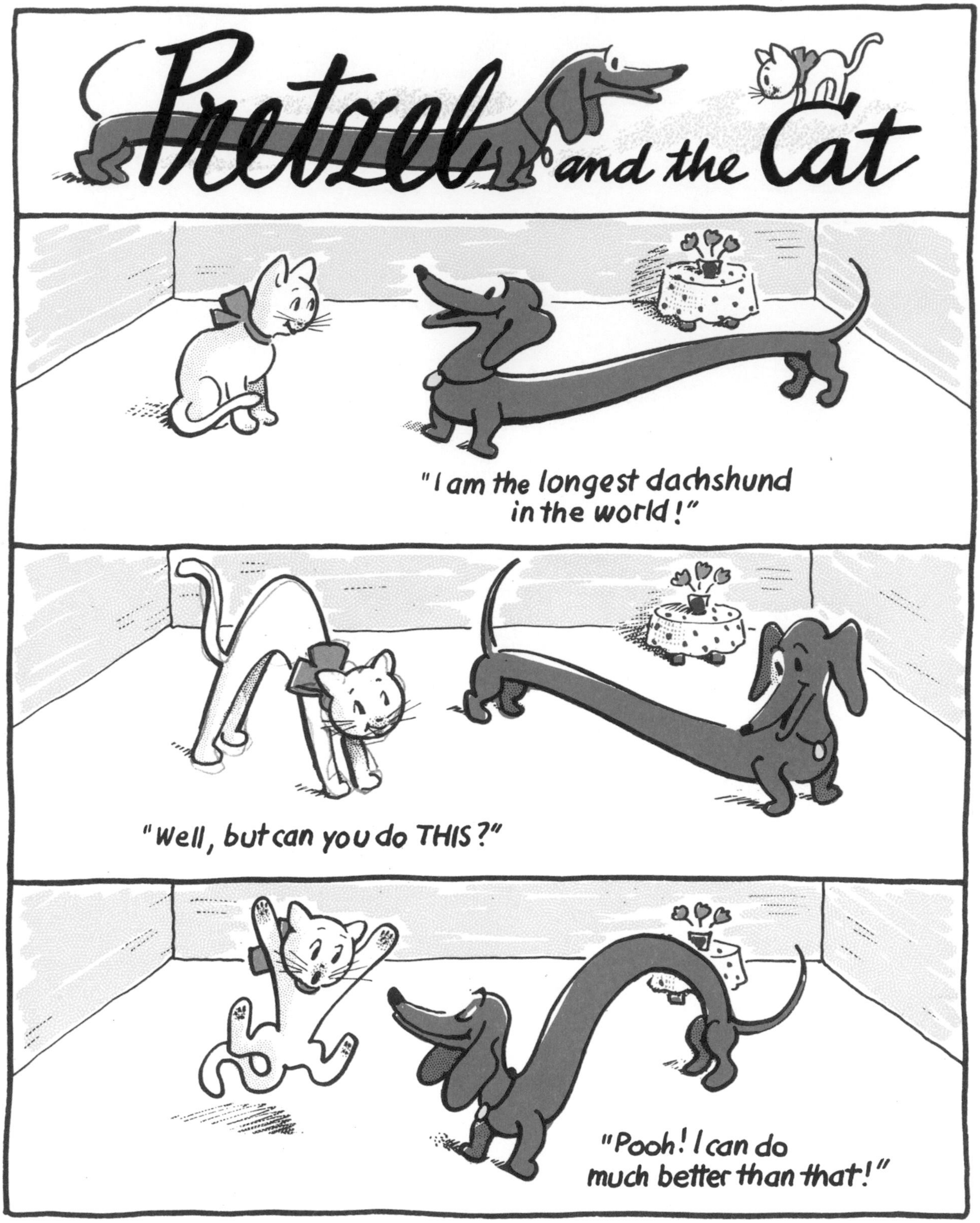
Pretzel and the Cat
"I am the longest dachshund in the world!"
"Well, but can you do THIS?"
"Pooh! I can do much better than that!"

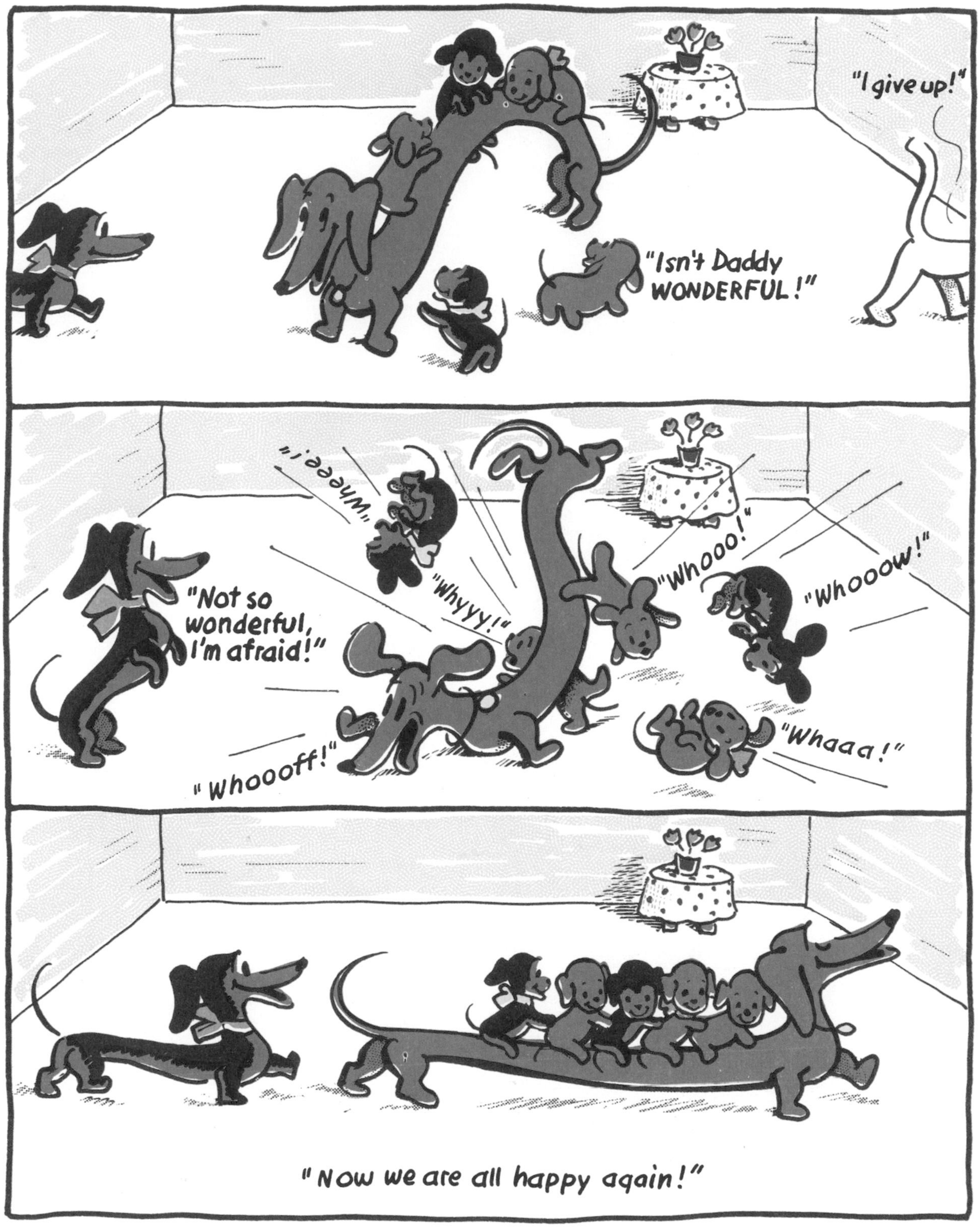
"I give up!"
"Isn't Daddy WONDERFUL!"
"Not so wonderful, I'm afraid!"
"Wheee!"
"Whyyy!"
"Whooo!"
"Whooow!"
"Whaaa!"
"Whoooff!"
"Now we are all happy again!"

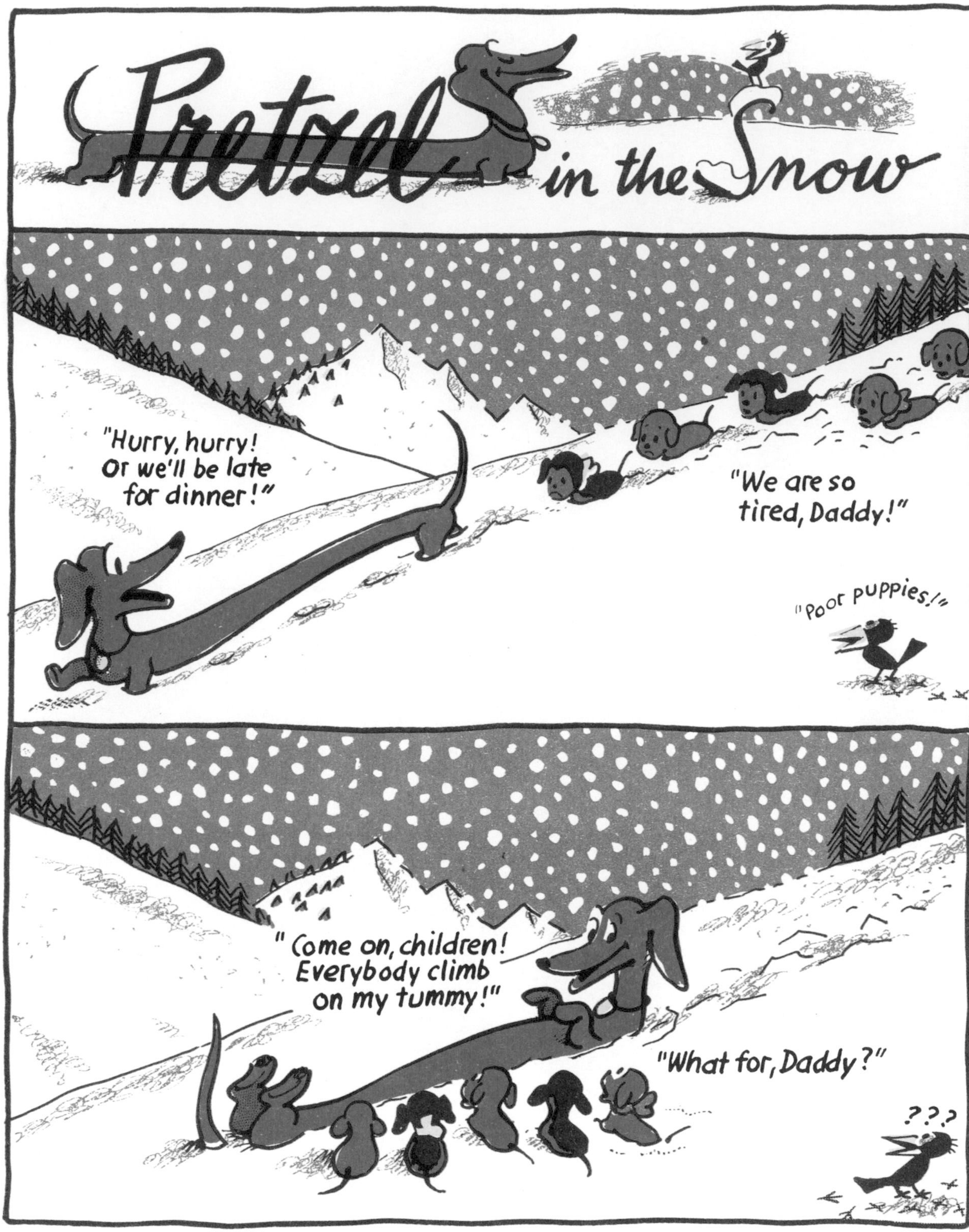
Pretzel in the Snow
"Hurry, hurry! Or we'll be late for dinner!"
"We are so tired, Daddy!"
"Poor puppies!"
"Come on, children! Everybody climb on my tummy!"
"What for, Daddy?"
???

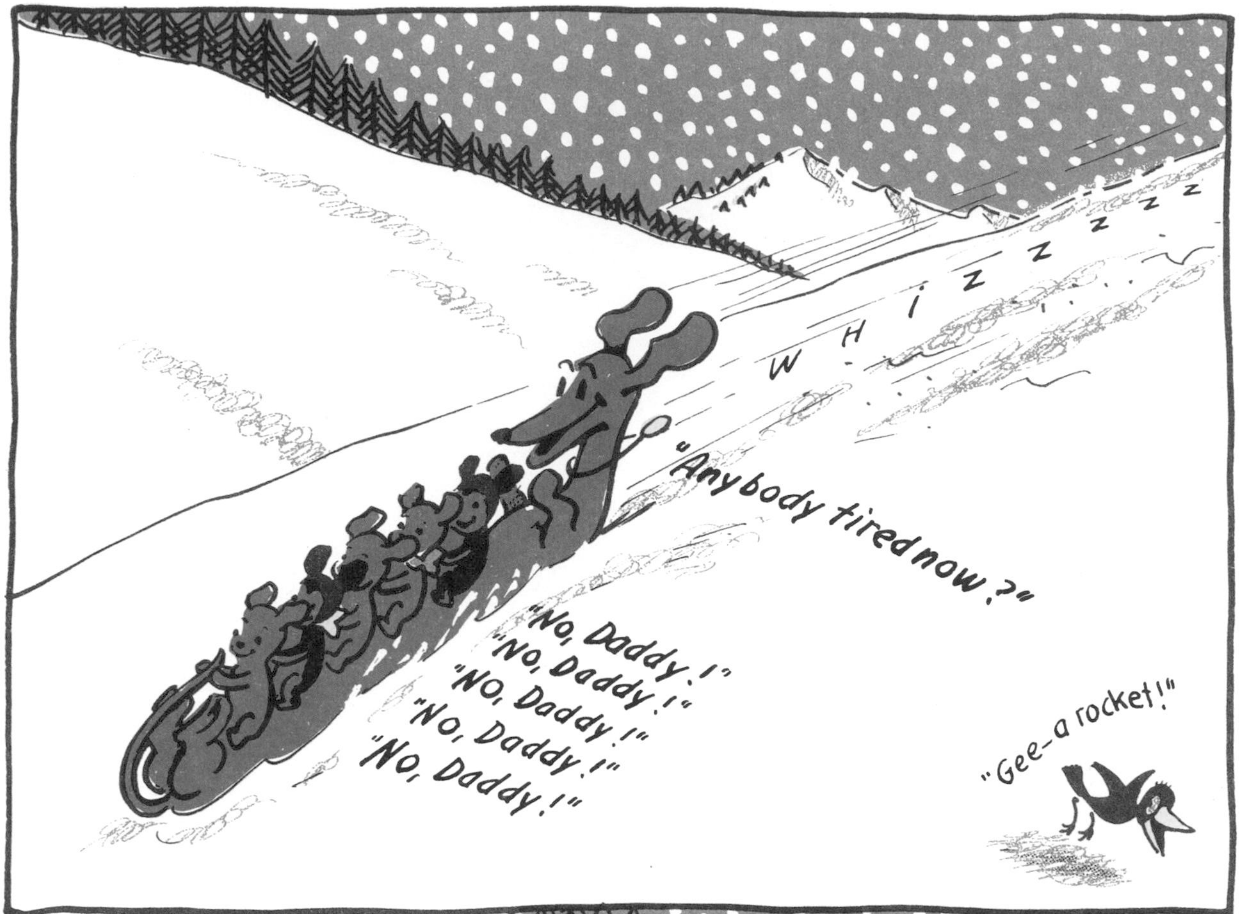

WHIZZZZZZZ
"Anybody tired now?"
"No, Daddy!"
"No, Daddy!"
"No, Daddy!"
"No, Daddy!"
"No, Daddy!"
"Gee—a rocket!"

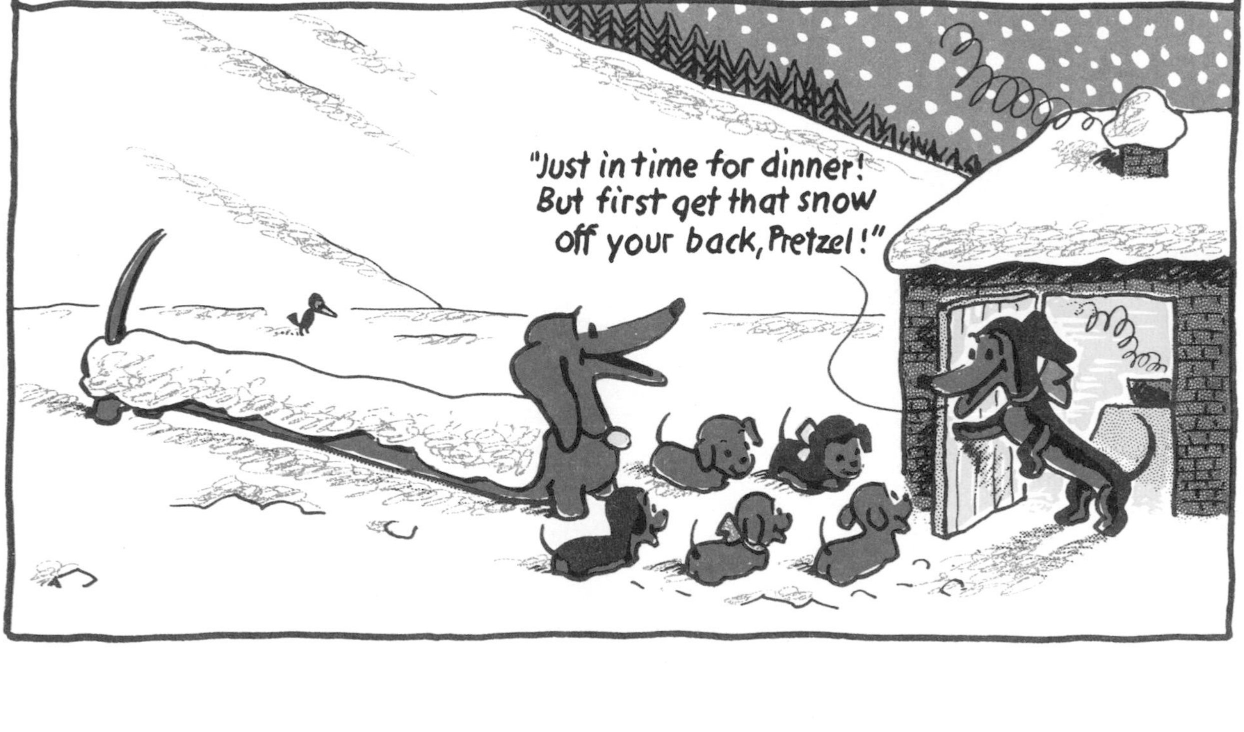

"Just in time for dinner! But first get that snow off your back, Pretzel!"

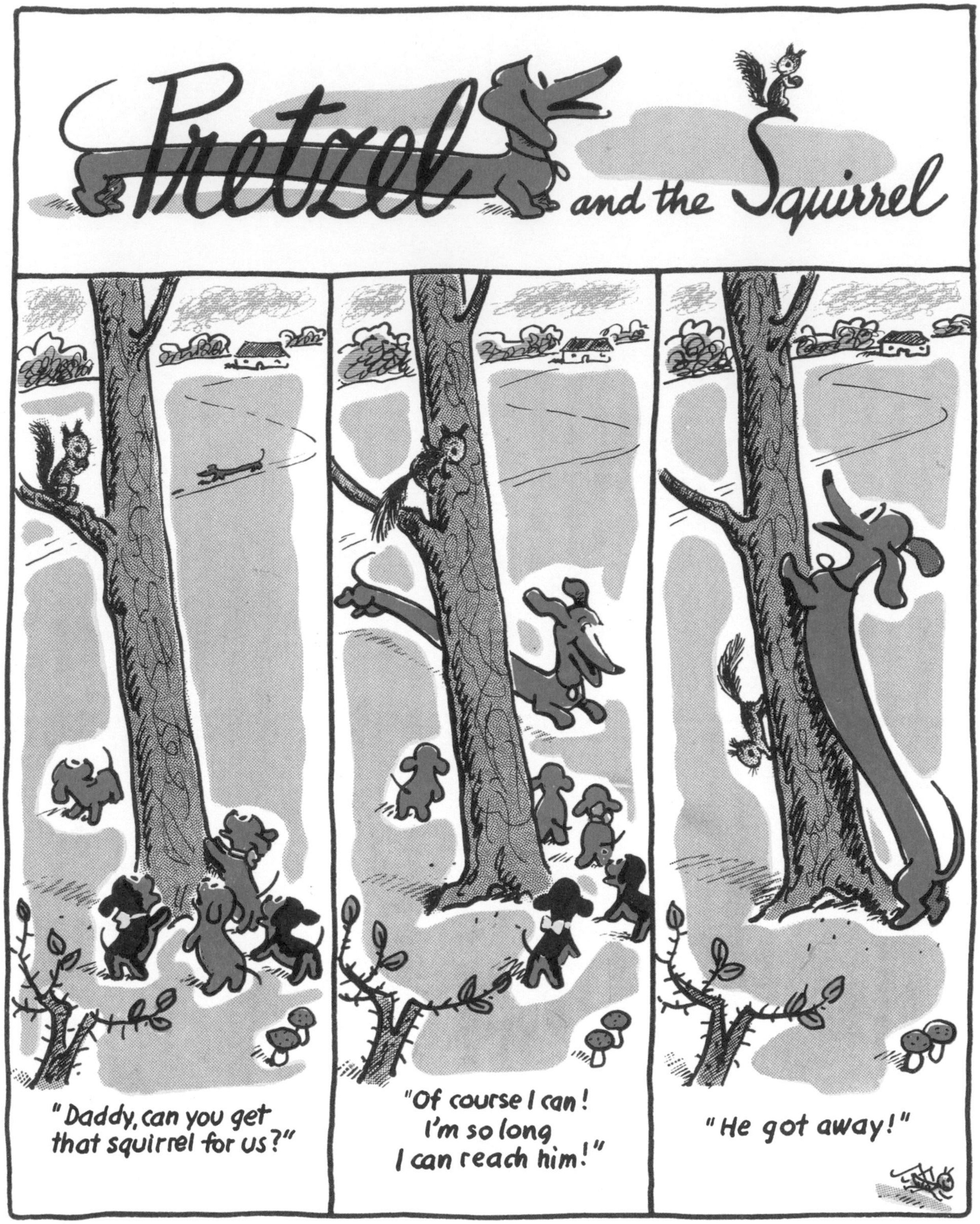
Pretzel and the Squirrel
"Daddy, can you get that squirrel for us?"
"Of course I can! I'm so long I can reach him!"
"He got away!"

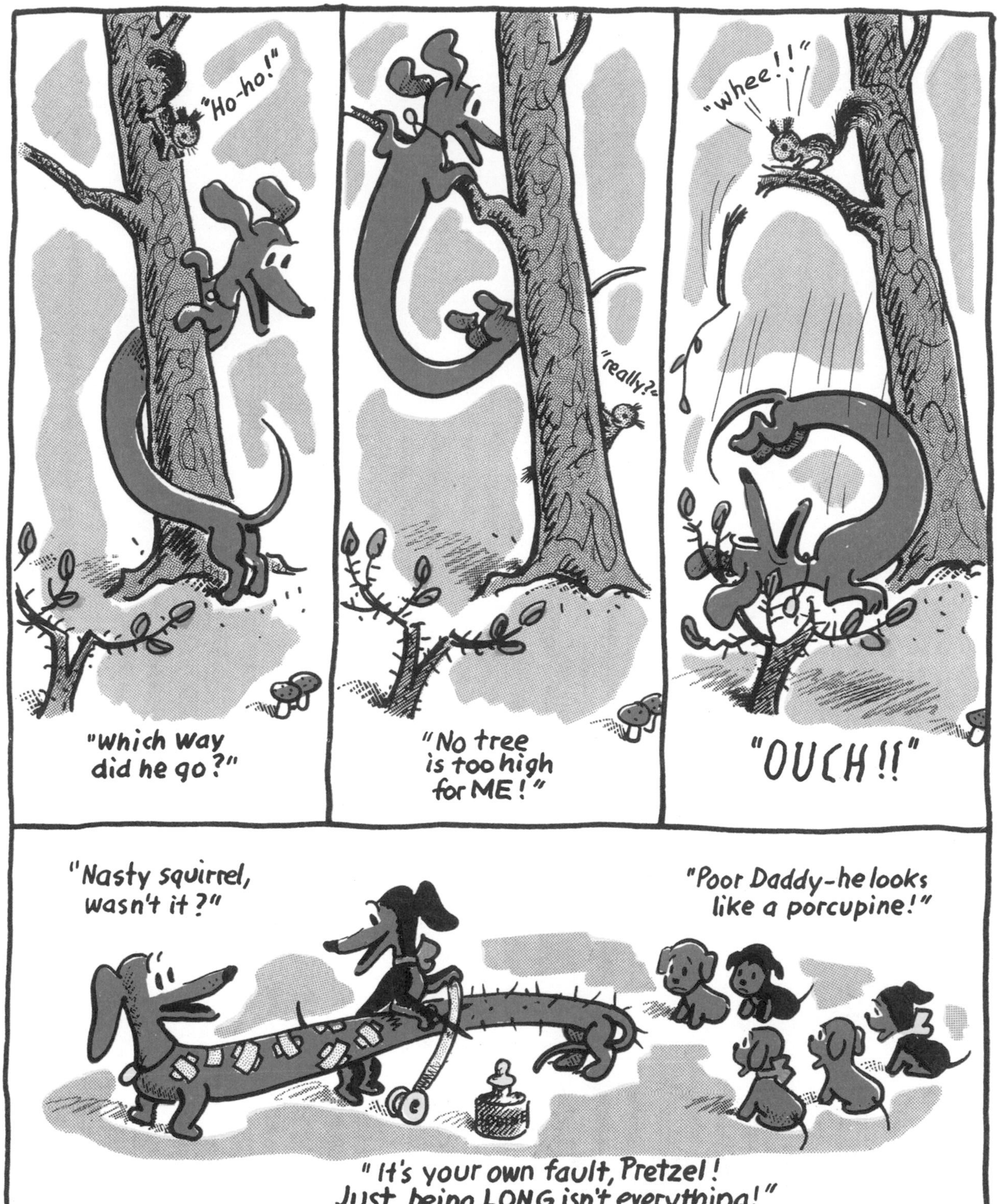
"Ho-ho!"
"Which way did he go?"
"No tree is too high for ME!"
"really?"
"whee!!"
"OUCH!!"
"Nasty squirrel, wasn't it?"
"Poor Daddy-he looks like a porcupine!"
"It's your own fault, Pretzel! Just being LONG isn't everything!"

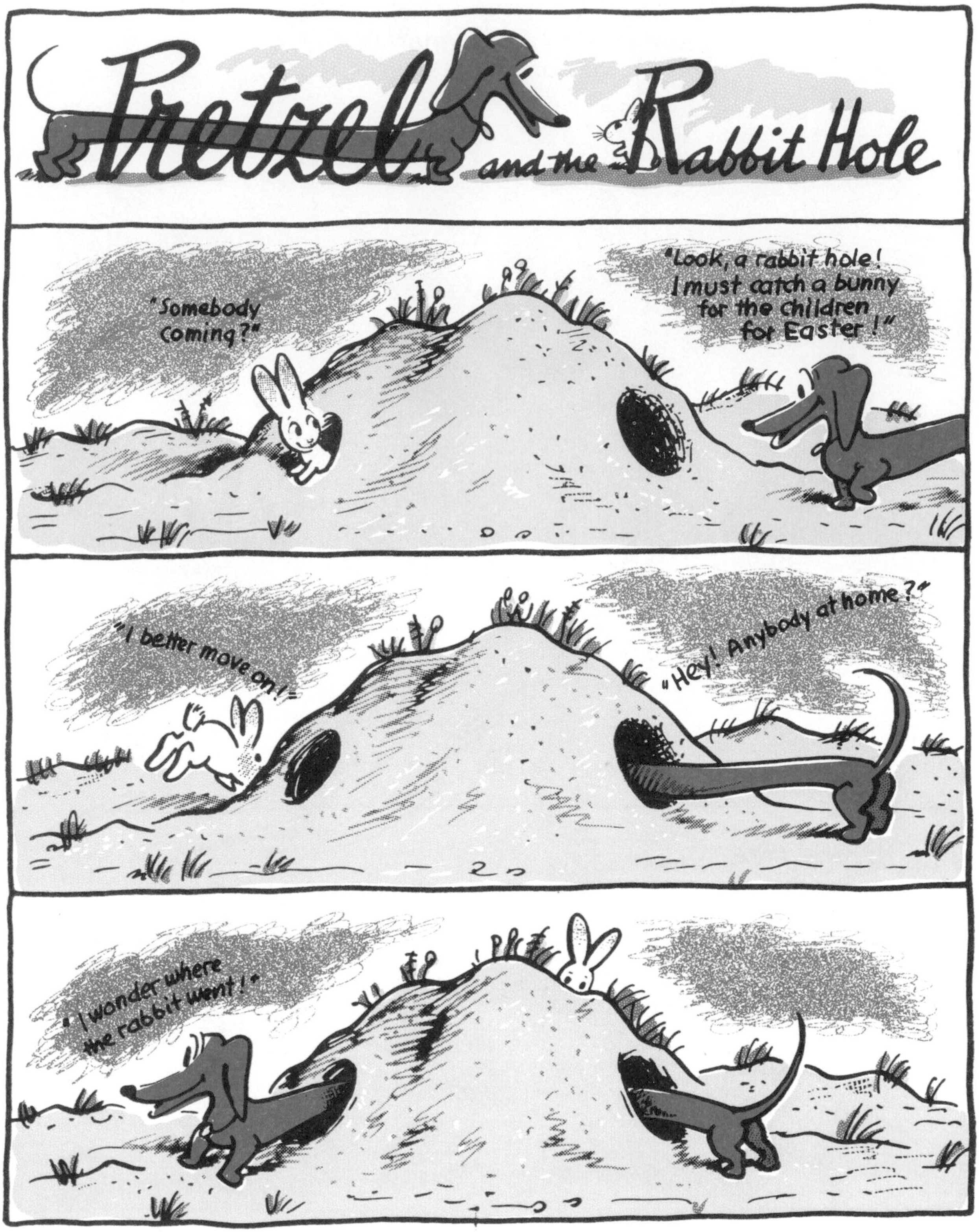
Pretzel and the Rabbit Hole
"Somebody coming?"
"Look, a rabbit hole! I must catch a bunny for the children for Easter!"
"I better move on!"
"Hey! Anybody at home?"
"I wonder where the rabbit went!"

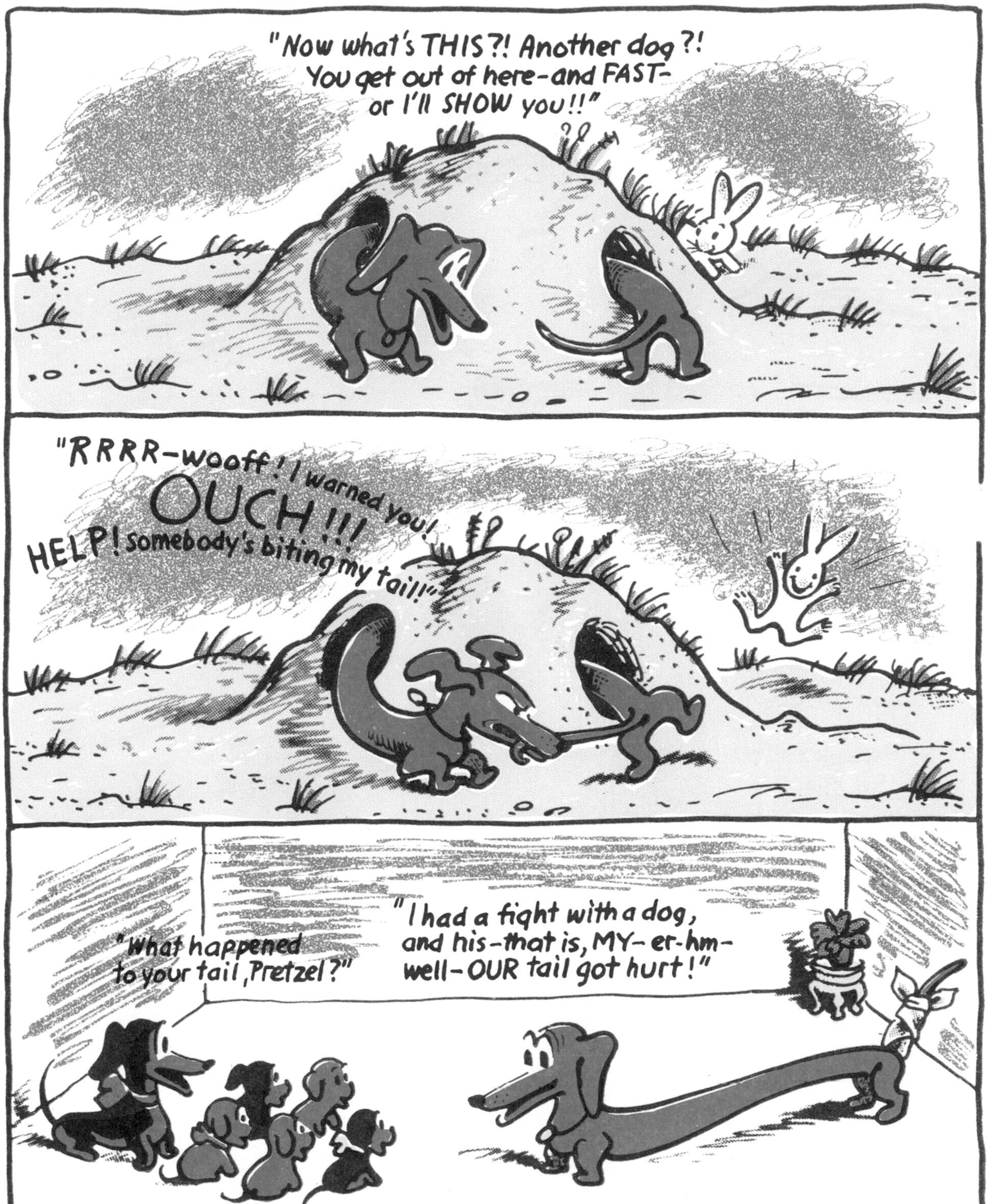
"Now what's THIS?! Another dog?! You get out of here-and FAST-or I'll SHOW you!!"
"RRRR-wooff! I warned you!
OUCH!!!
HELP! somebody's biting my tail!"
"What happened to your tail, Pretzel?"
"I had a fight with a dog, and his-that is, MY-er-hm-well-OUR tail got hurt!"

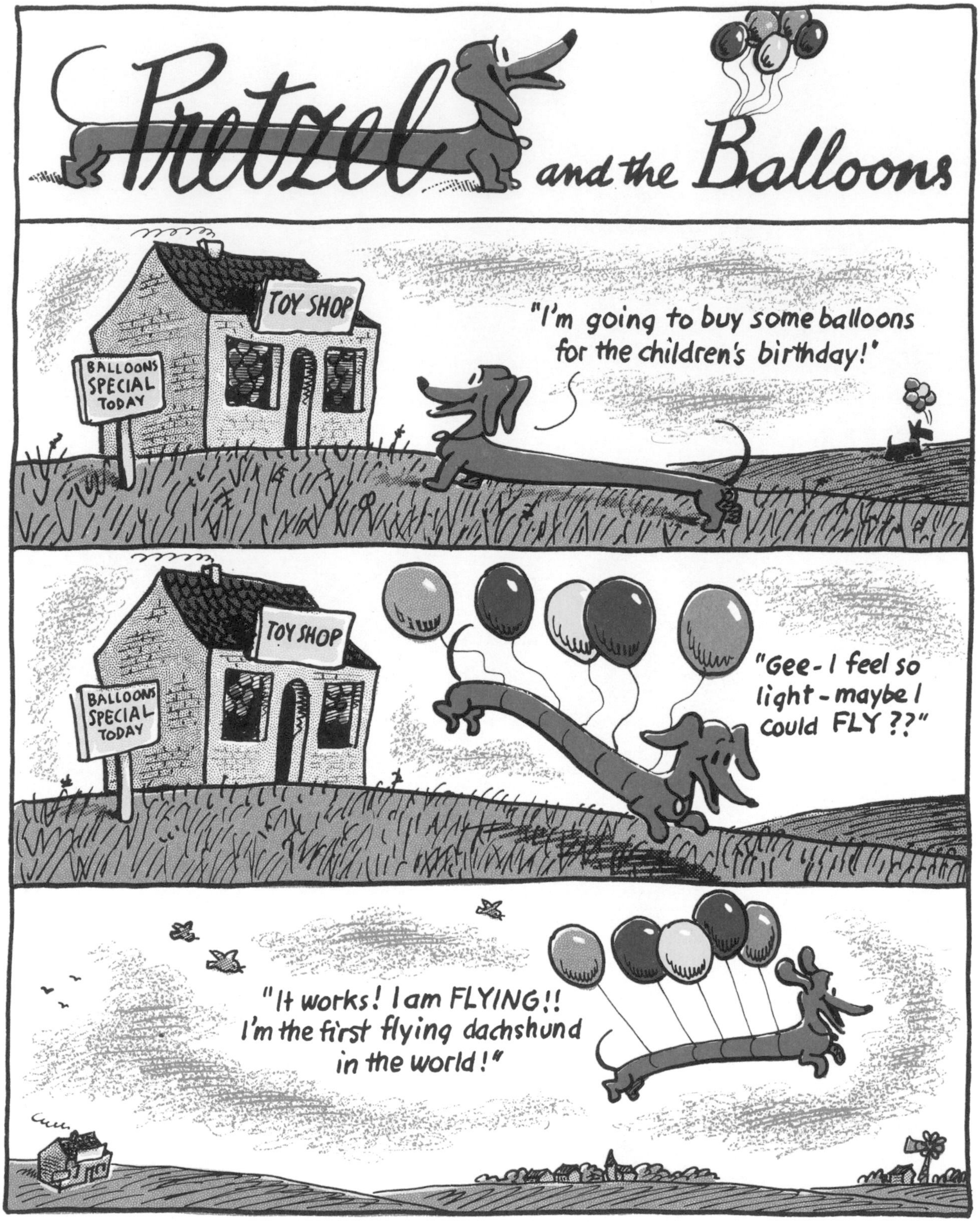
Pretzel and the Balloons
TOY SHOP
BALLOONS SPECIAL TODAY
"I'm going to buy some balloons for the children's birthday!"
TOY SHOP
BALLOONS SPECIAL TODAY
"Gee - I feel so light - maybe I could FLY??"
"It works! I am FLYING!! I'm the first flying dachshund in the world!"

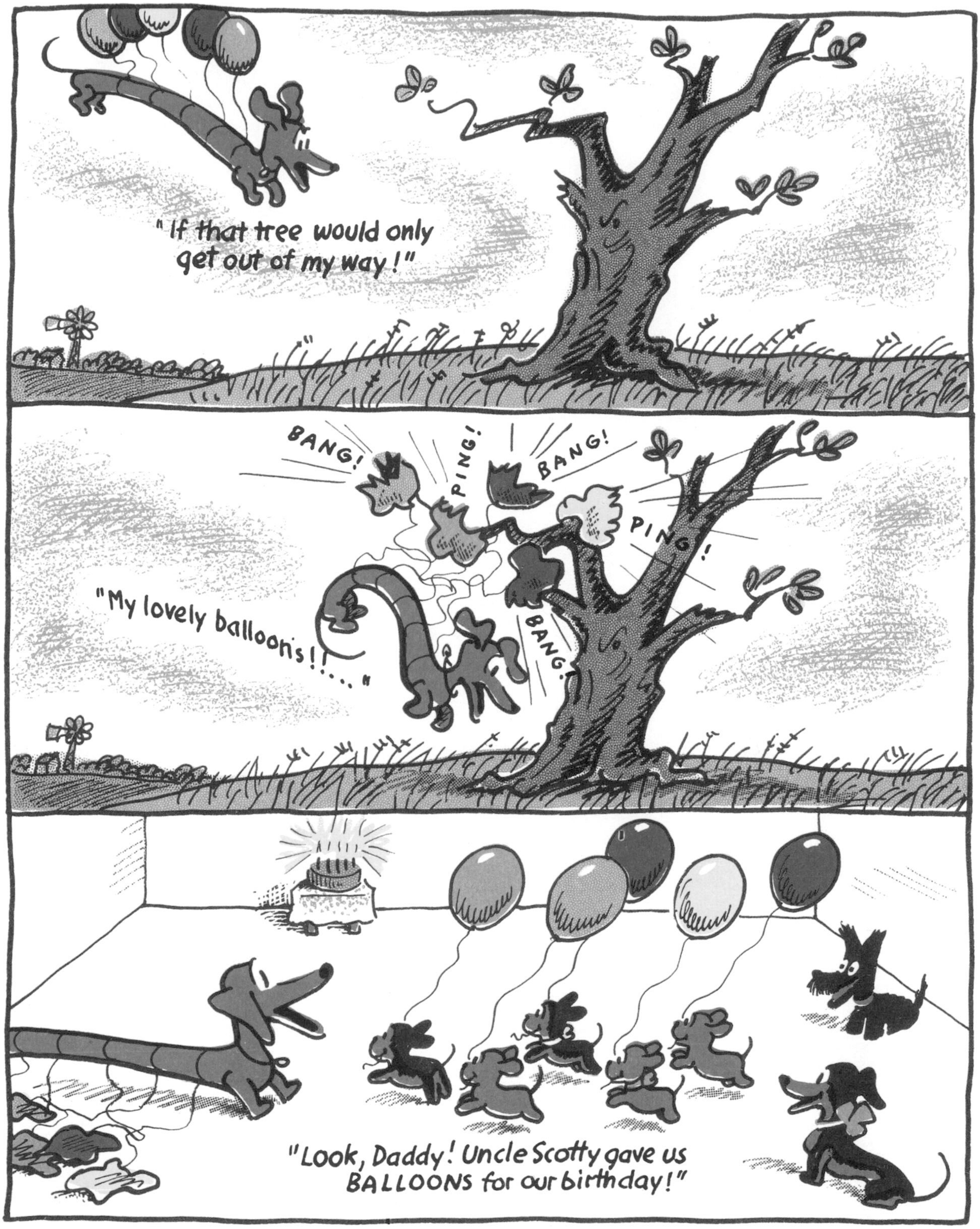
"If that tree would only get out of my way!"
BANG!
PING!
BANG!
PING!
"My lovely balloons!!...."
BANG!
"Look, Daddy! Uncle Scotty gave us BALLOONS for our birthday!"

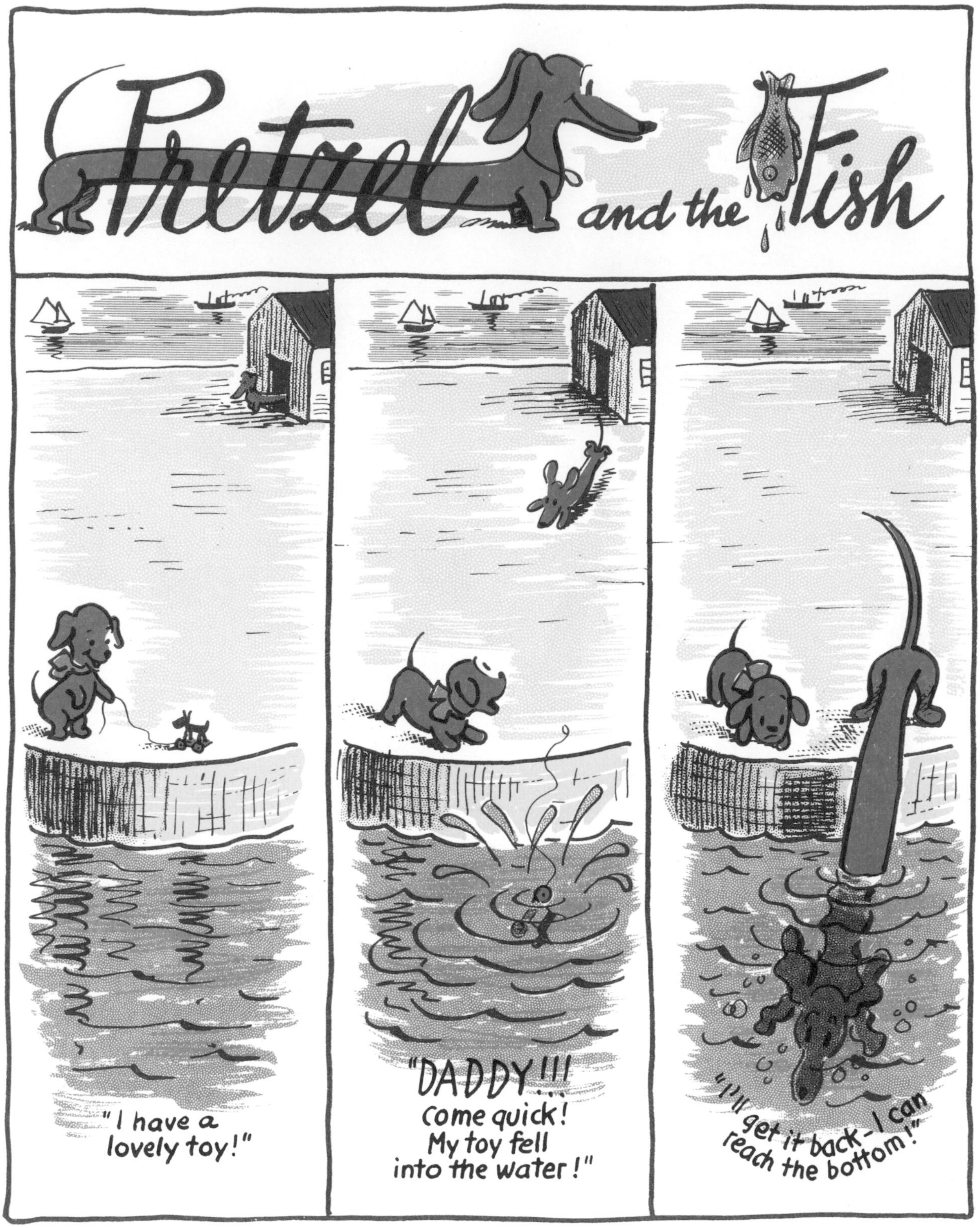
Pretzel and the Fish
"I have a lovely toy!"
"DADDY!!! Come quick! My toy fell into the water!"
"I'll get it back—I can reach the bottom!"

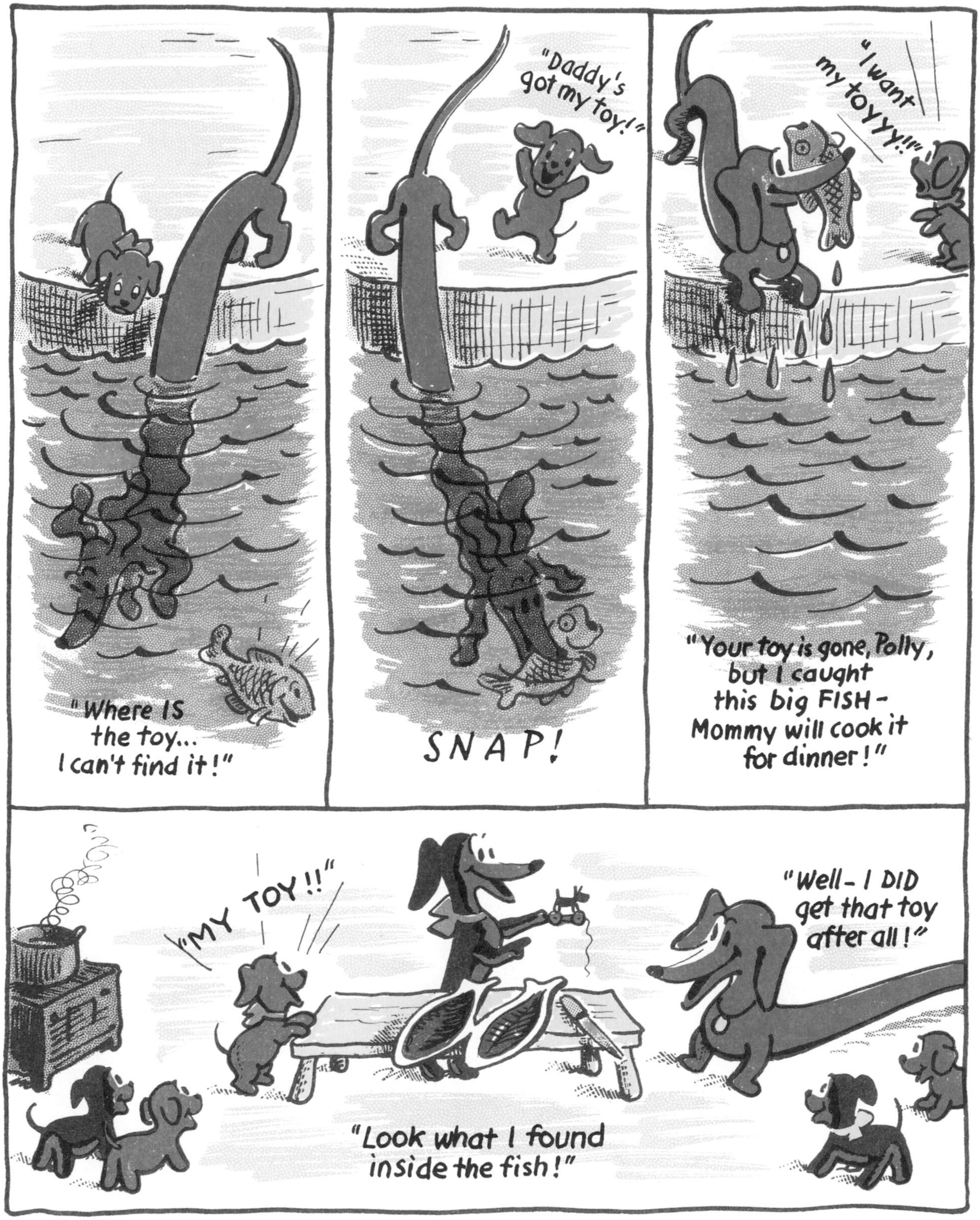
"Where IS the toy... I can't find it!"
"Daddy's got my toy!"
SNAP!
"I want my toyyy!!"
"Your toy is gone, Polly, but I caught this big FISH - Mommy will cook it for dinner!"
"MY TOY!!"
"Look what I found inside the fish!"
"Well - I DID get that toy after all!"

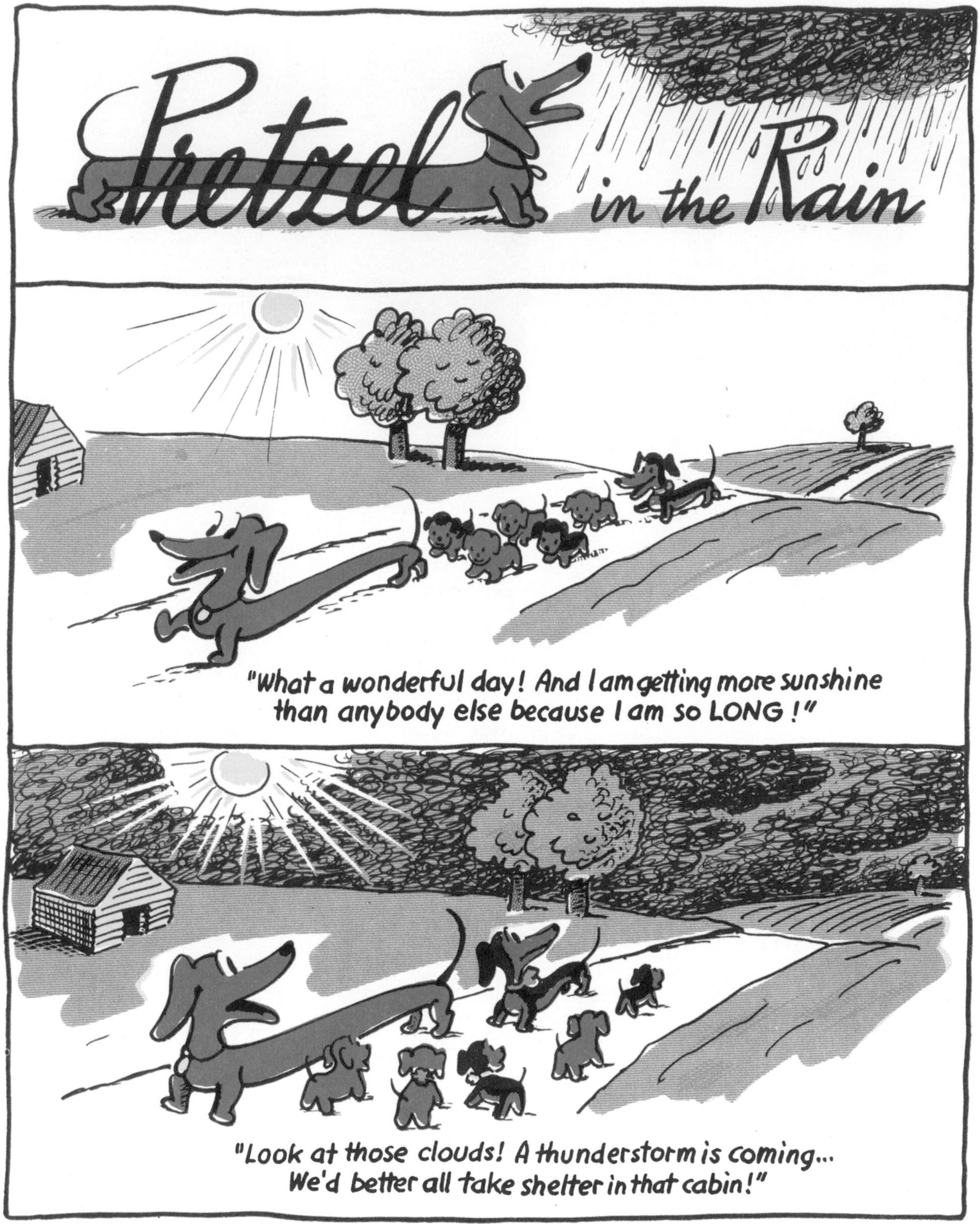
Pretzel in the Rain
"What a wonderful day! And I am getting more sunshine than anybody else because I am so LONG!"
"Look at those clouds! A thunderstorm is coming... We'd better all take shelter in that cabin!"

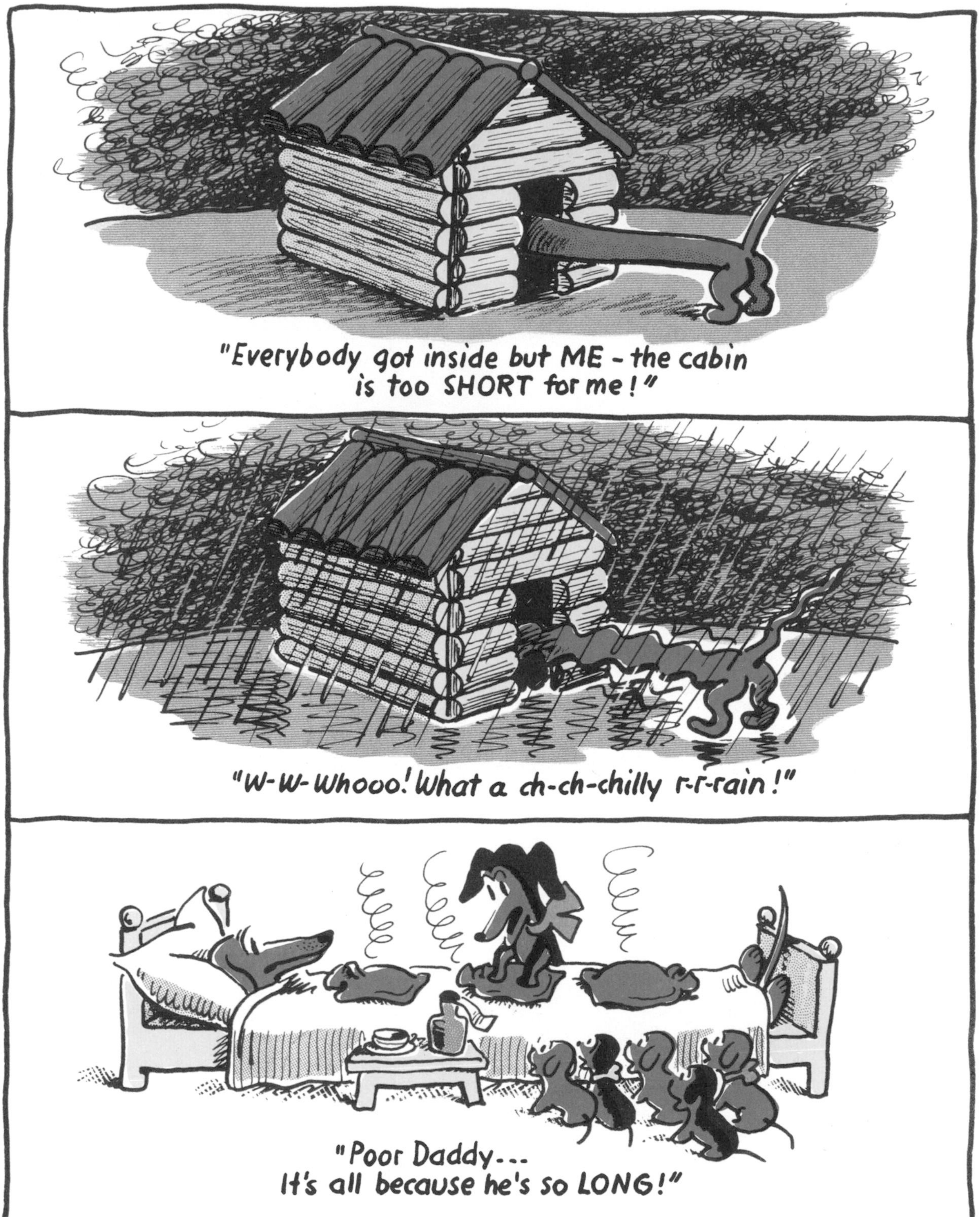
"Everybody got inside but ME - the cabin is too SHORT for me!"
"W-W-Whooo! What a ch-ch-chilly r-r-rain!"
"Poor Daddy...
It's all because he's so LONG!"

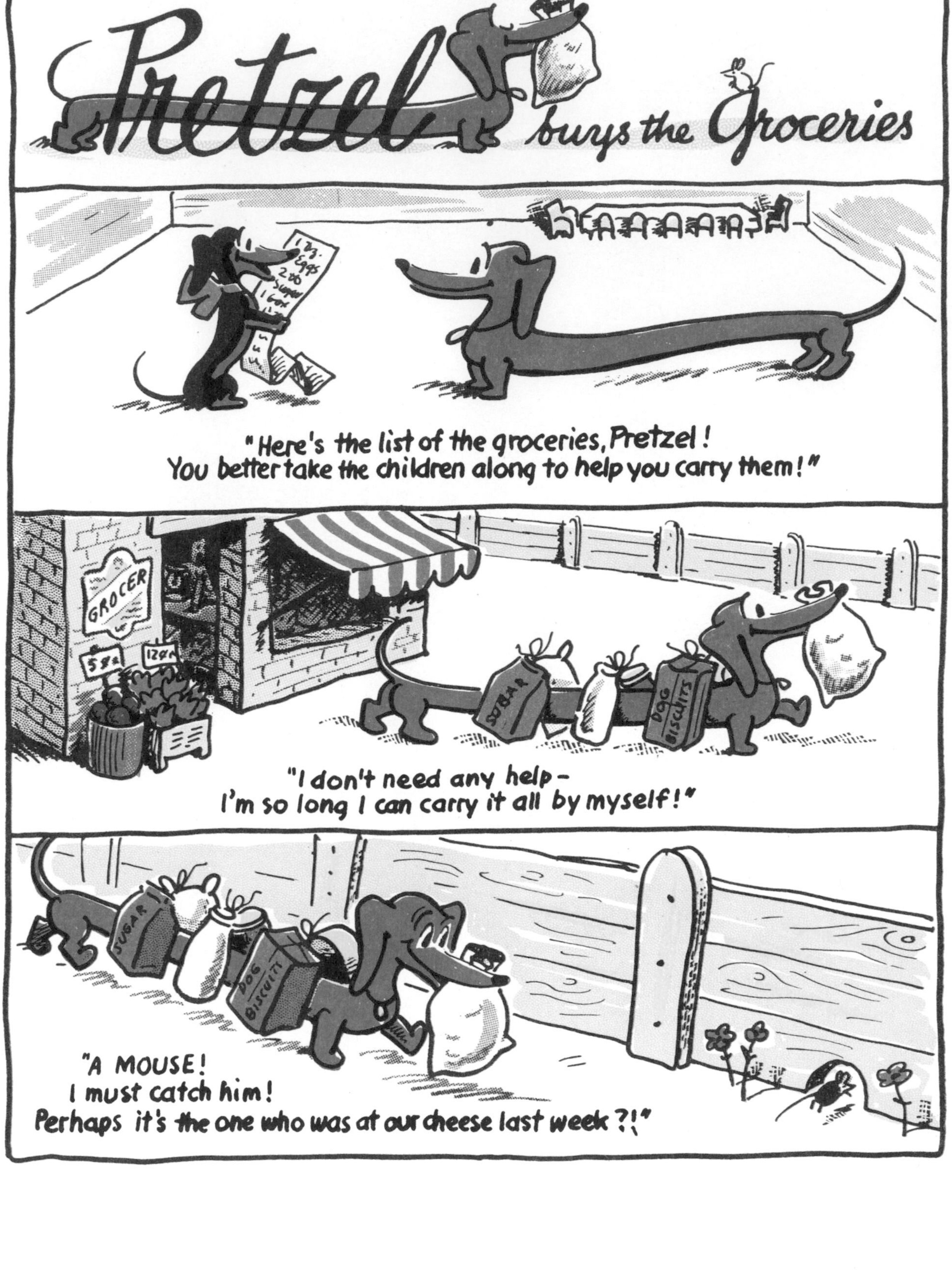
Pretzel buys the Groceries
"Here's the list of the groceries, Pretzel!
You better take the children along to help you carry them!"
GROCER
SUGAR
DOG BISCUITS
"I don't need any help -
I'm so long I can carry it all by myself!"
SUGAR
DOG BISCUITS
"A MOUSE!
I must catch him!
Perhaps it's the one who was at our cheese last week?!"

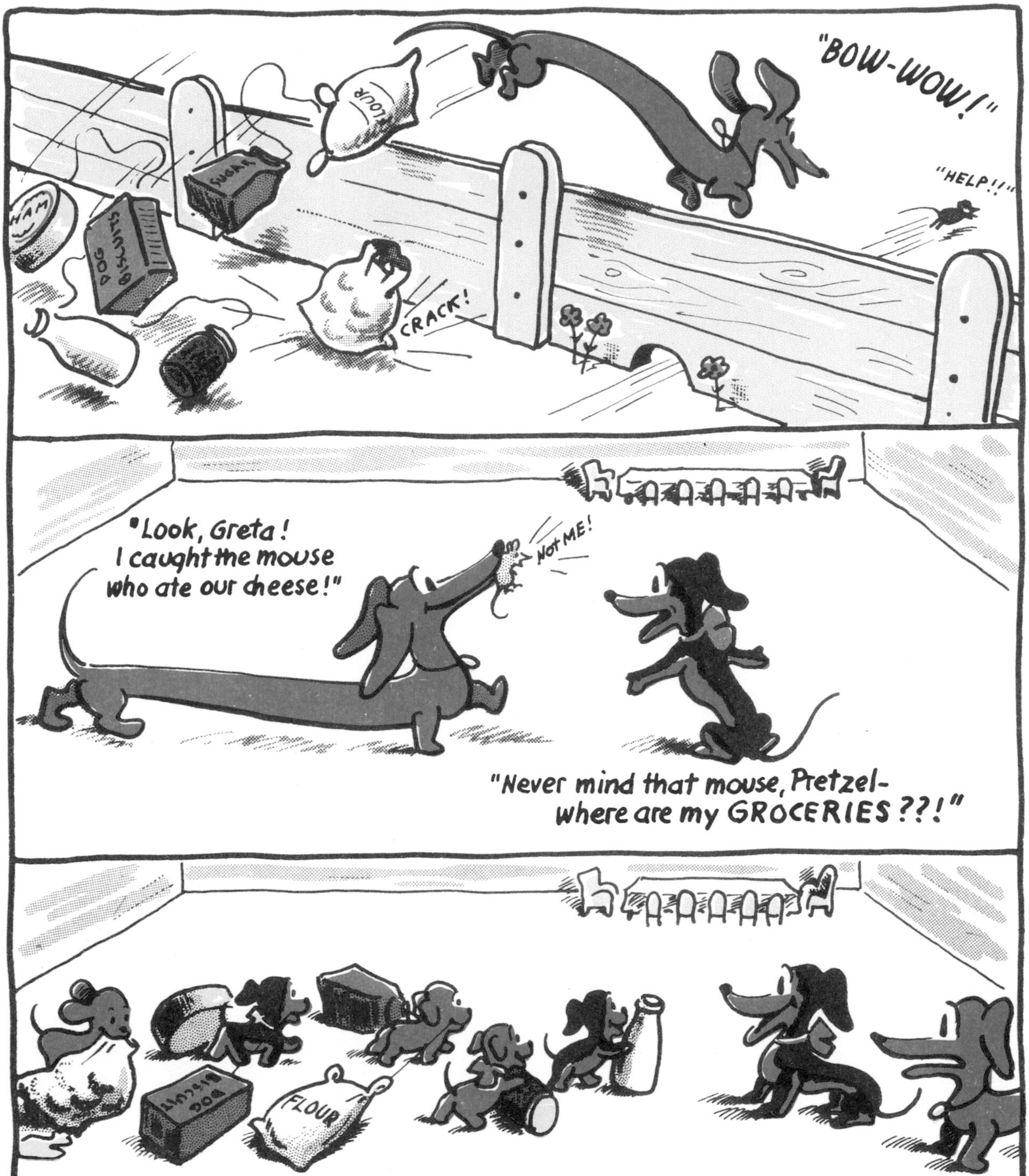
"BOW-WOW!"
"HELP!!"
FLOUR
SUGAR
HAM
DOG BISCUITS
CRACK!
"Look, Greta! I caught the mouse who ate our cheese!"
NOT ME!
"Never mind that mouse, Pretzel- where are my GROCERIES ??!"
DOG BISCUIT
FLOUR
"Here they are, Mommy! Somebody left them outside the garden fence!"

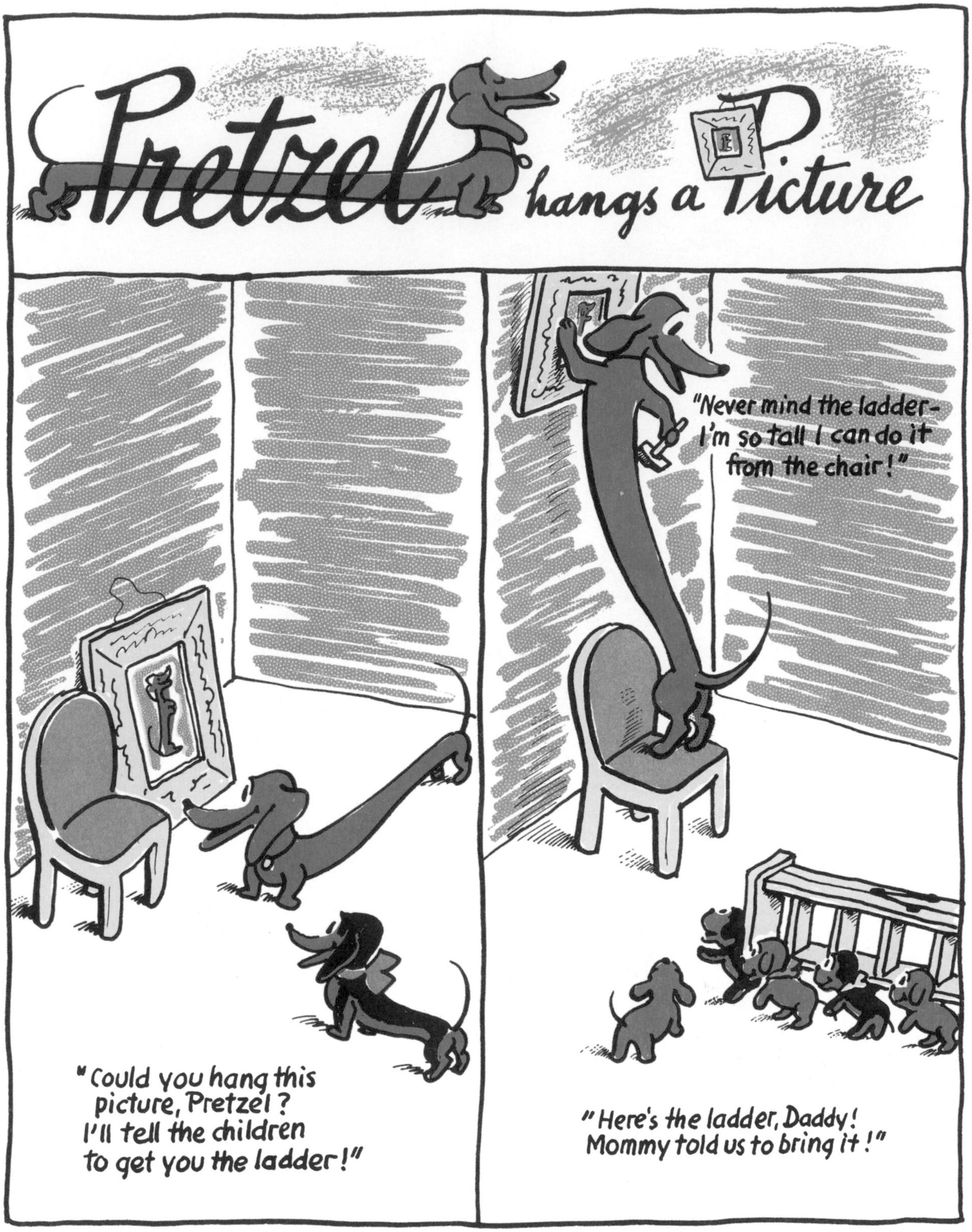
Pretzel hangs a Picture
"Could you hang this picture, Pretzel? I'll tell the children to get you the ladder!"
"Never mind the ladder- I'm so tall I can do it from the chair!"
"Here's the ladder, Daddy! Mommy told us to bring it!"

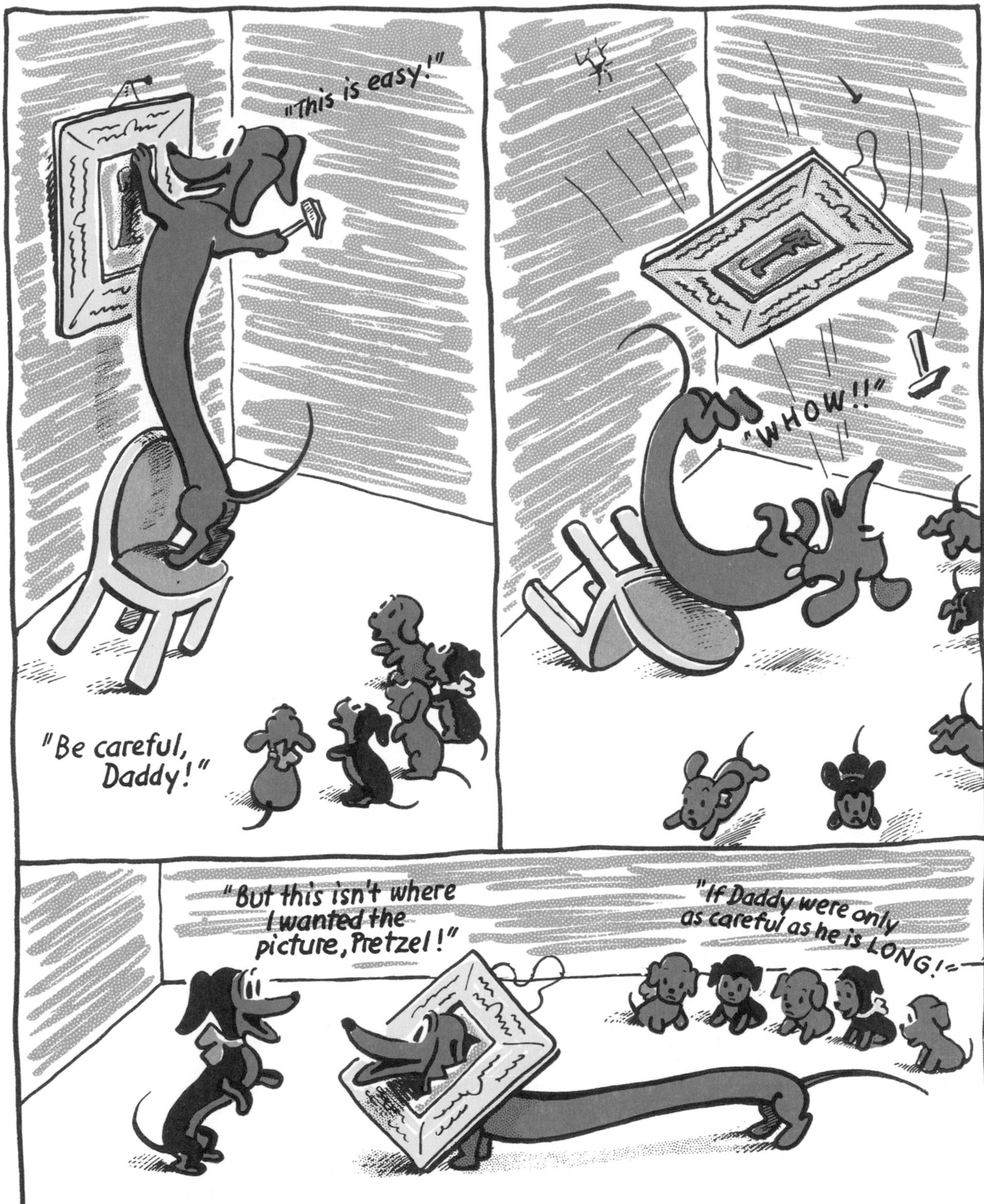
"This is easy!"
"Be careful, Daddy!"
"WHOW!!"
"But this isn't where I wanted the picture, Pretzel!"
"If Daddy were only as careful as he is LONG!"

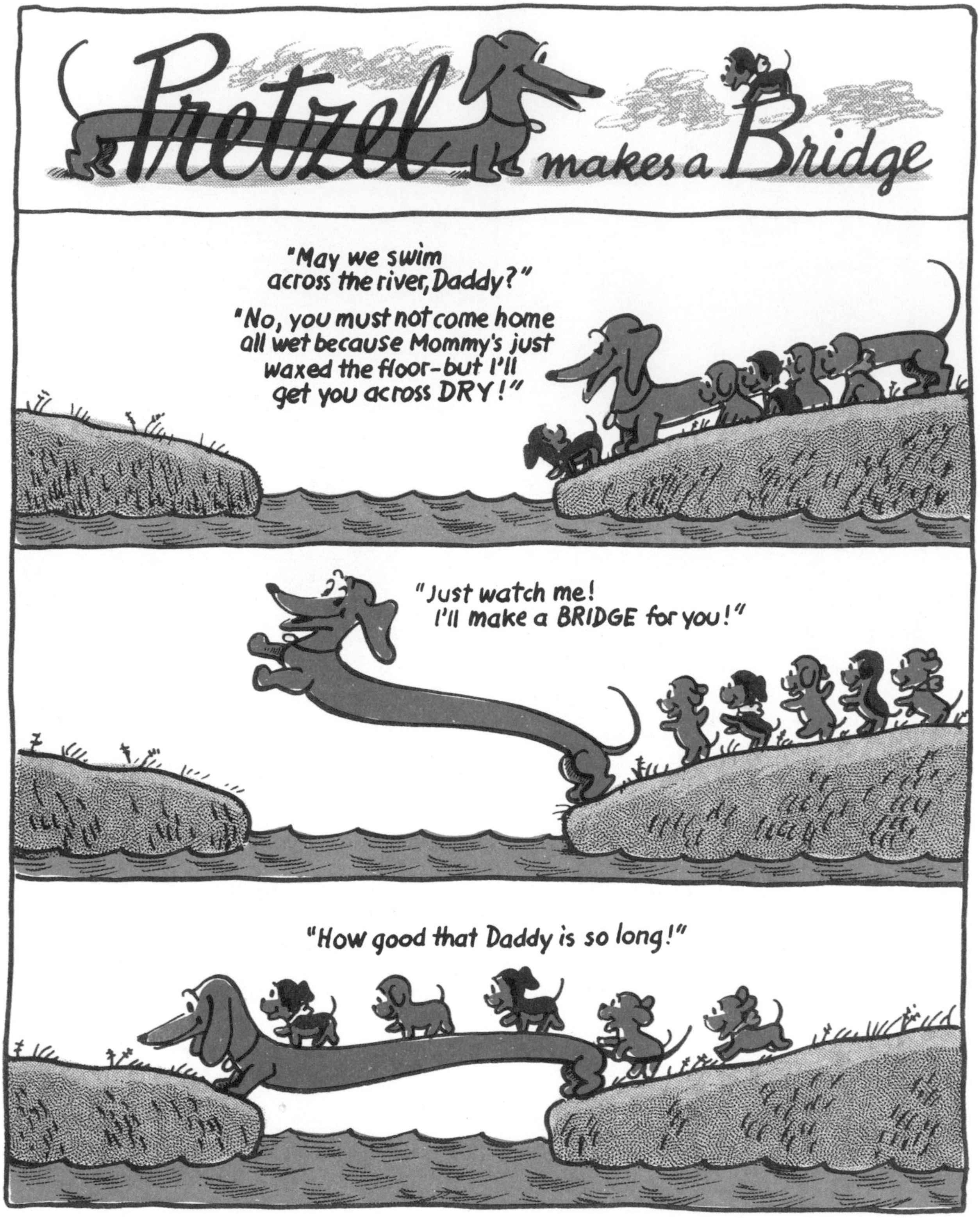

Pretzel makes a Bridge
"May we swim across the river, Daddy?"
"No, you must not come home all wet because Mommy's just waxed the floor—but I'll get you across DRY!"
"Just watch me! I'll make a BRIDGE for you!"
"How good that Daddy is so long!"

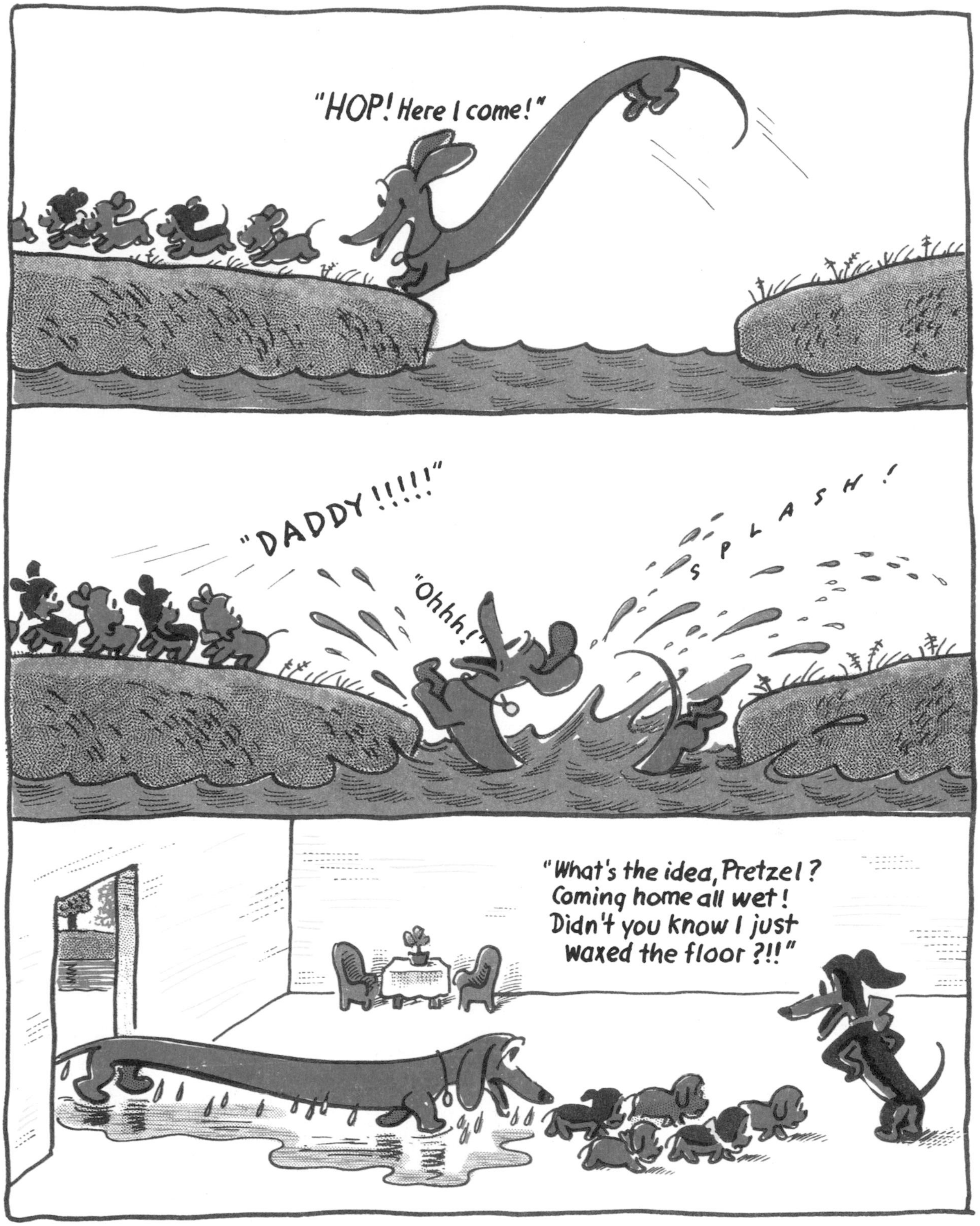
"HOP! Here I come!"
"DADDY!!!!!"
SPLASH!
"Ohhh!"
"What's the idea, Pretzel? Coming home all wet! Didn't you know I just waxed the floor?!!"

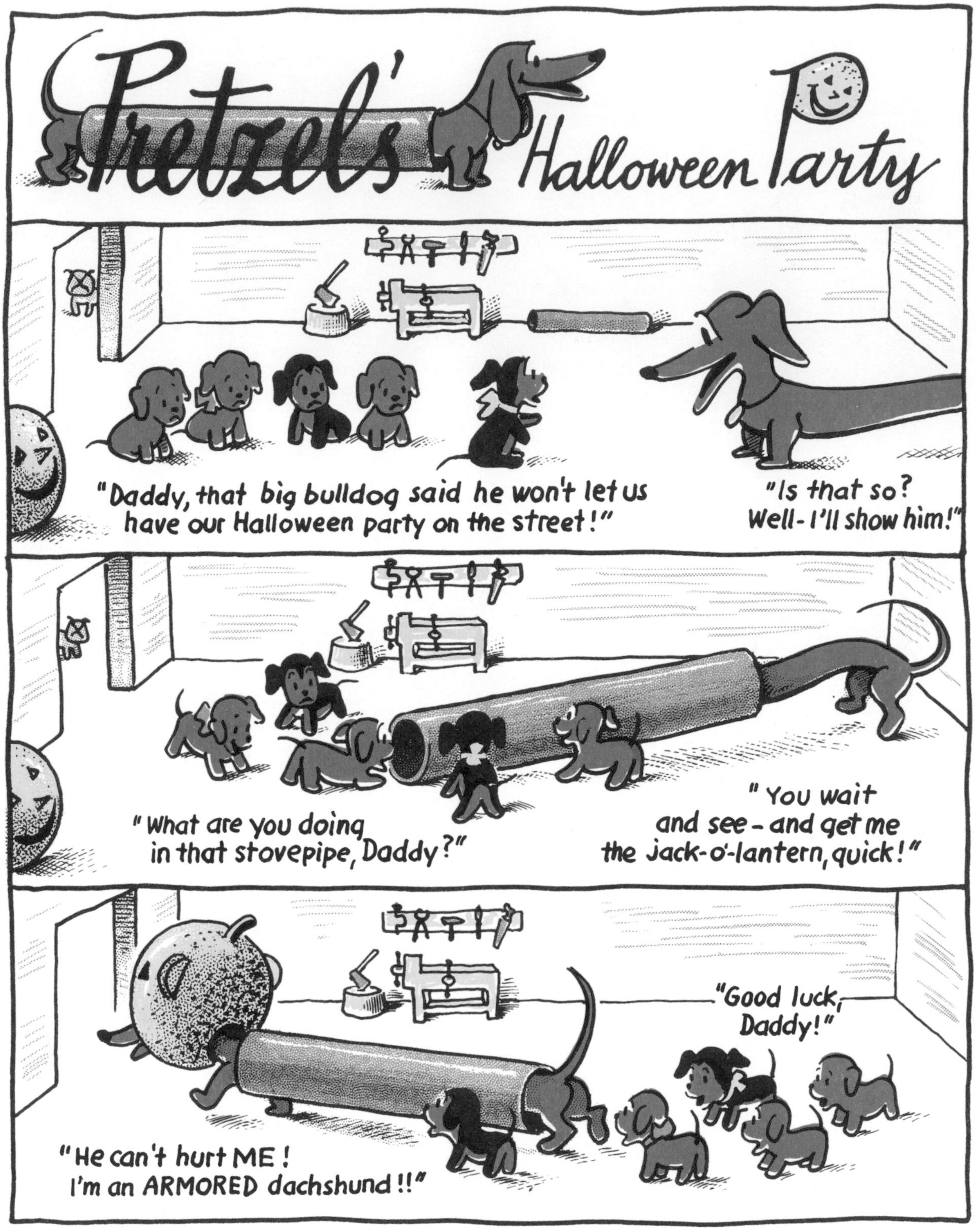
Pretzel's Halloween Party
"Daddy, that big bulldog said he won't let us have our Halloween party on the street!"
"Is that so? Well- I'll show him!"
"What are you doing in that stovepipe, Daddy?"
"You wait and see - and get me the jack-o'-lantern, quick!"
"Good luck, Daddy!"
"He can't hurt ME! I'm an ARMORED dachshund!!"

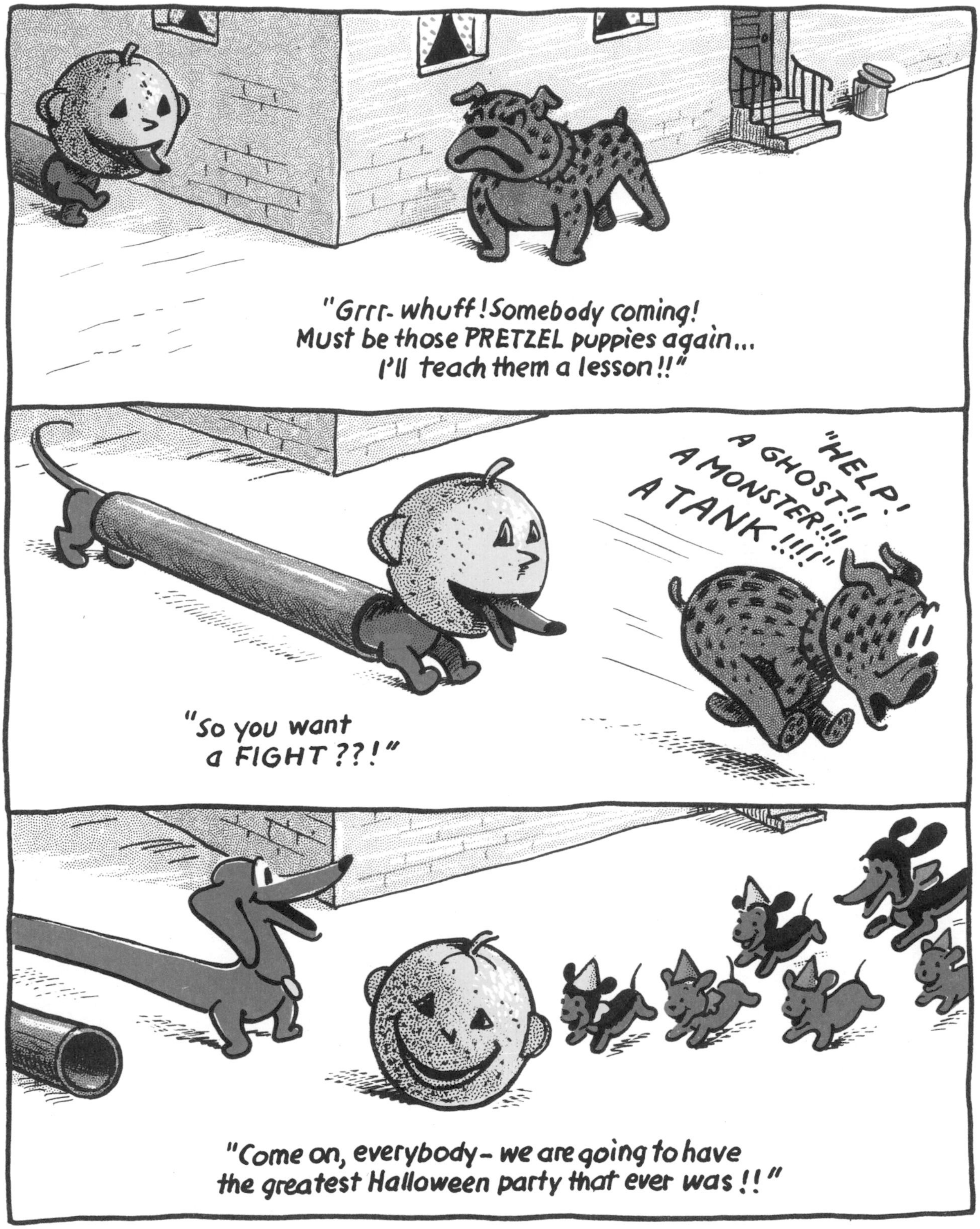
"Grrr- whuff! Somebody coming!
Must be those PRETZEL puppies again...
I'll teach them a lesson!!"
"So you want
a FIGHT??!"
"HELP!
A GHOST!!
A MONSTER!!!
A TANK!!!!"
"Come on, everybody- we are going to have
the greatest Halloween party that ever was!!"

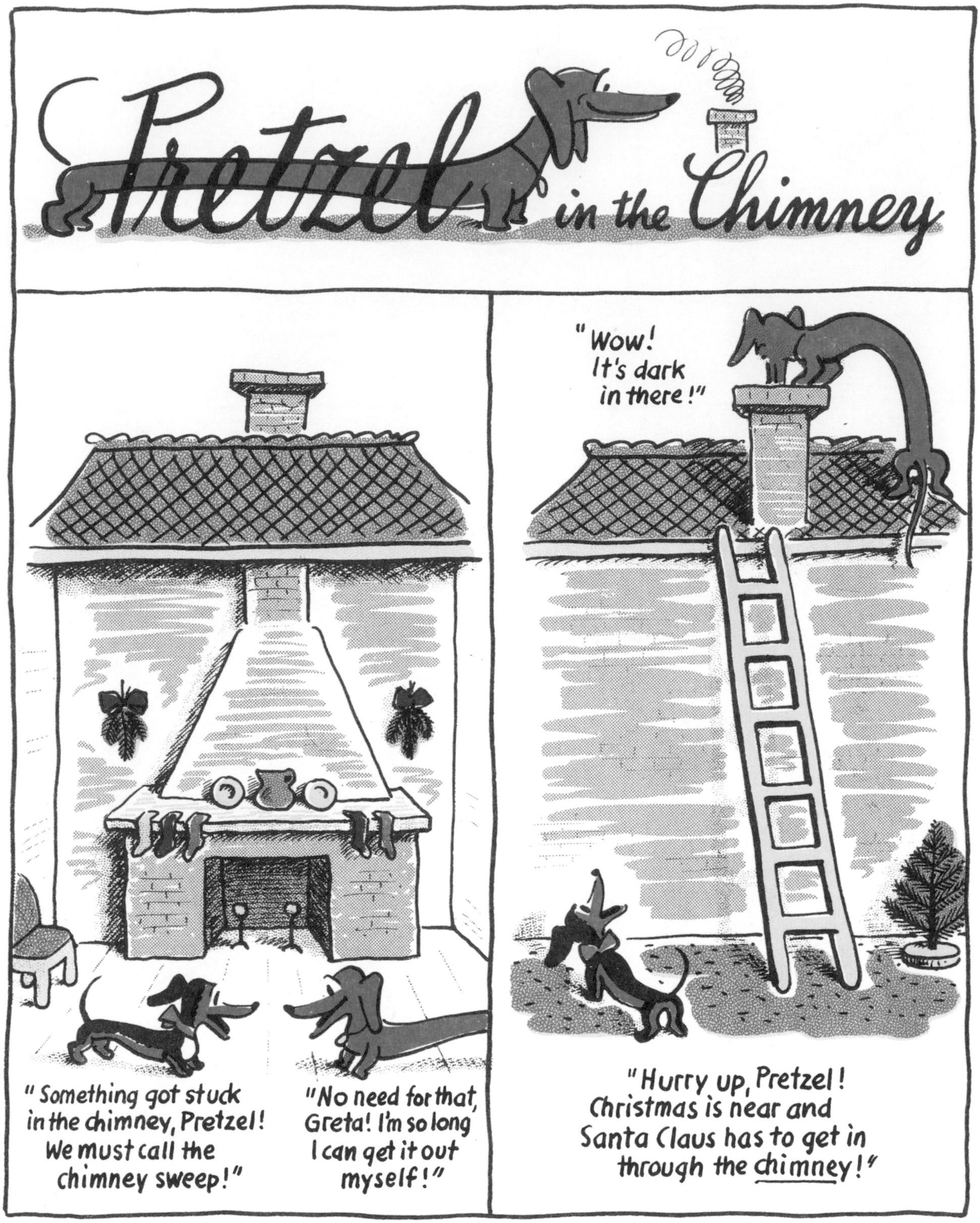
Pretzel in the Chimney
"Something got stuck in the chimney, Pretzel! We must call the chimney sweep!"
"No need for that, Greta! I'm so long I can get it out myself!"
"Wow! It's dark in there!"
"Hurry up, Pretzel! Christmas is near and Santa Claus has to get in through the chimney!"

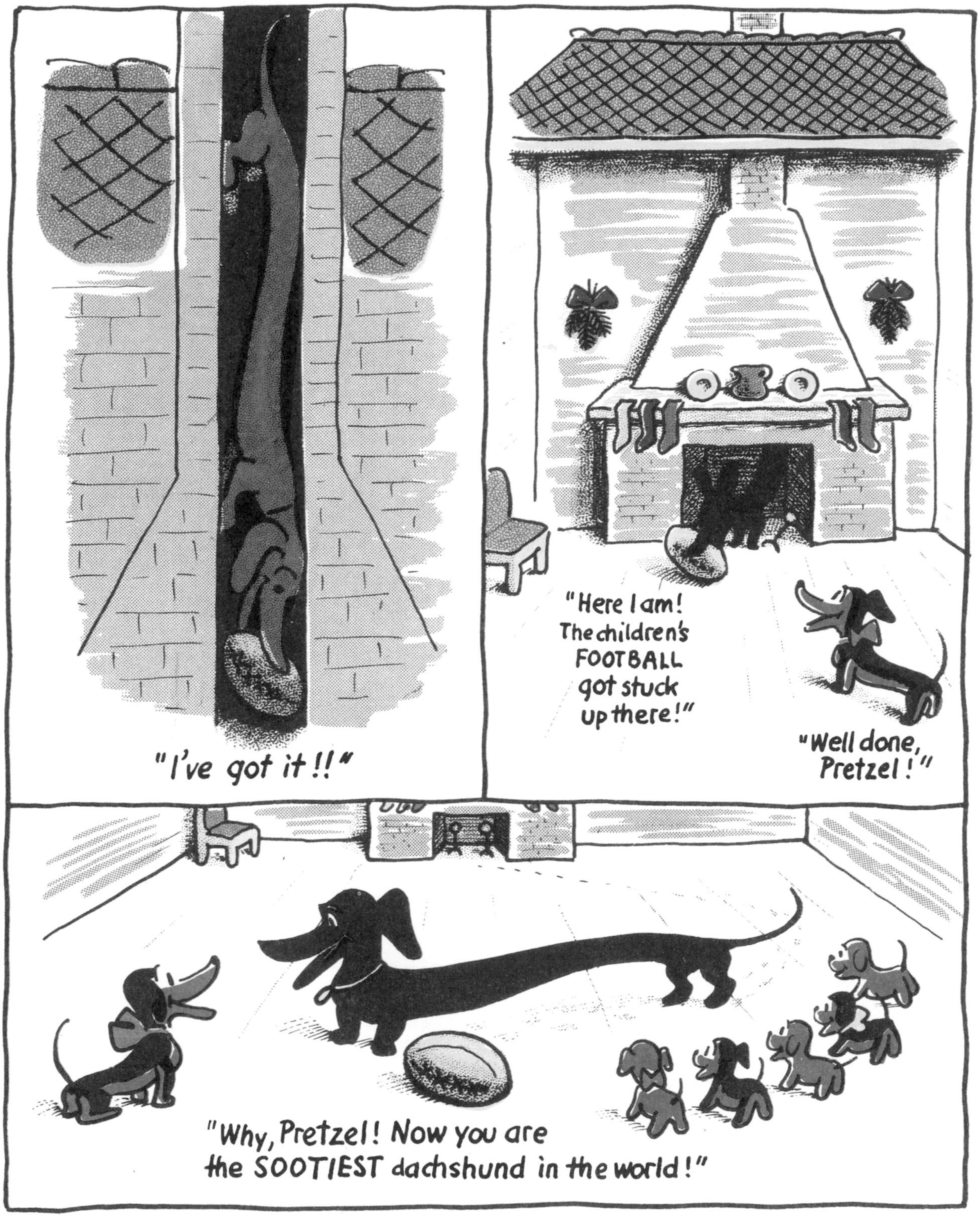
"I've got it!!"
"Here I am! The children's FOOTBALL got stuck up there!"
"Well done, Pretzel!"
"Why, Pretzel! Now you are the SOOTIEST dachshund in the world!"

That's all –
goodbye!

Copyright © 1946 by Margret and H. A. Rey. Copyright renewed 1974 by Margret and H. A. Rey.
Originally published in hardcover by Harper & Brothers, 1946.

For information about permission to reproduce selections from this book,
write to trade.permissions@hmhco.com or to Permissions,
Houghton Mifflin Harcourt Publishing Company, 3 Park Avenue, 19th Floor, New York, New York 10016.

hmhbooks.com

The text of this book is hand lettered.

ISBN: 978-0-358-46826-4 hardcover
ISBN: 978-0-358-65959-4 paperback

Printed in Italy
1
4500836211